When I Were a Meerkat...

When I Were a Meerkat...

Andrew Davies

PORTICO

First published in the United Kingdom in 2011 by
Portico Books
10 Southcombe Street
London
W14 0RA

An imprint of Anova Books Company Ltd

ISBN 13: 978-1-907554-36-0

A CIP catalogue record for this book is available from
the British Library.

10 9 8 7 6 5 4 3 2 1

Reproduction by Rival Colour Ltd.
Printed and bound by Everbest Printing Co. Ltd, China

This book can be ordered direct from the publisher.
Contact the marketing department, but try your bookshop first.

www.anovabooks.com

Contents

We Loved Our Dustbins

It were tough growing up as meerkat.

We didn't have two farthings to rub together.

Even when we did, we kept dropping them out of paws.

They used to tell us, "Where there's muck, there's brass".

But we could only find muck.

6

One of our favourite games was hide and seek.
We used to love hiding in dustbins...

Except we ruined it by poking our heads out every five minutes to look round.

Something always gave us away.

11

Even though we always got caught there were something comforting about a dustbin... it were warm, smelly and dark.

Like a cinema without the film.

13

Of course there were hell to pay from
our Mum when we got home.
"Straight in bath with you m'lad."
Even if it weren't Sunday.

Mums and Dads

Most of us were brought up by mums who we adored.
She were bedrock of family and stood for no nonsense.
Absolutely no taking worms up to your bedroom –
eat 'em on table like everyone else.

...not that we had bedrooms mind.

17

Some mums had to work, so most of looking after was done by sisters or friends of family.

19

And there's some that had four very ugly mums.
Obsessed with hats.

21

Posh folk loved to adopt a meerkat.
They'd go along to orphanage, or pick out a really
cute one from big basket of orphans they used
to tout round streets.

Then they'd stick em in pram the size of
a Bentley Continental and go up the park
to show off to all the other posh mums.

Nanny would push, obviously.
Those things weighed a ton.

There's some as got their own personal nurse maid,
a bed to themselves, clothes that hadn't been worn
by half the street and shop-bought beetles.
It were cloud cuckoo land - the minute they grew into
awkward teenagers they were sent to work in kitchen.

27

No, our mums were top.
If we stepped out of line we knew we'd get
a leatherin', so we learnt our manners.
No foul language, no catching moths, no vigorous
scratching or grooming fur in front of guests.

29

A lot of the dads used to work for colliery.

It had been same for generations, we had natural skill underground. Pit bosses knew that.

Wherever you found coal, you'd find meerkats.
From Ebbw vale to vale of York we'd be scrabbling around,
digging out the black gold for meagre wage.
Pit for pittance me dad used to say.
He worked at mill.

35

When Dad got home from work, first thing
he wanted was a nice sit-down, cuppa and smoke.
And if he were feeling fancy, a tasty bit of scorpion pie.
Even if it were only dried scorpions, not live ones.

School Weren't Much Fun

They tell you that school days are 'happiest days of your life'... Which means that rest of your life's going to be pretty chuffin' miserable.

Mrs Boothroyd would never believe the excuse, "our sister buried me homework".

Girls
Put your bags here

Heating in our school was only ever turned on once.
In 1936.

Maths were nightmare. Other kids could count up to ten on their fingers…We only had eight.

43

Our classmates could be so cruel.
Yeah, go on, have a laff at the stupid meerkat...
In time we learned that kake, kooking, kar, kow,
kotton and krumble didn't start with a 'k'.

45

red

There was the odd swot, but we didn't talk to them.

You were never quite certain what were going
to happen with school nurse. Was it going to be
a painful jab or a gentle rummage for nits?

Colin were anxious about it but Arthur couldn't care less.

49

Some of the teachers we had were great.
They held you spellbound, in awe, hanging on
their every word.

51

And some of them were vicious, like Sister Hepplewhite, who'd administer 'the cat' for failing to name all seven disciples – or around that number.

53

Still, we had our fun.
Conkers were great in autumn.

As long as you could stop yourself
from eating them.

The thrill of owning your own bike was immense.
It may have been third-hand and rusty but
you could show it off by cycling to school.
It weren't quite so enjoyable when Mum panicked
and hung a sign on your back.

When it came to sport, cricket were always a bit of a mystery.

And if we played footer, it were always,
"stick the meerkat in goal!"
And then you'd have to stand in puddle for ninety
minutes and take blame for any goal that went in.

Most fun of all was going out in
Mrs Ollerenshawe's car of an afternoon.
We lost a few when she started doing handbrake turns,
but they soon pulled you out of hedge.

You Learned Lots in Spare Time

To be honest, you learned as much as you did at school when you were out and about with mates.

You learned not to ask if you could eat all the worms in their apples.

You learned which games were chuffin' pointless.

You learned to get to football match early,
or get passed over heads of crowd.

Though sometimes, even if you did get there early,
it could be a struggle to see...

And at least in them days they didn't rob you blind with official club shirts. Your nan could knit you complete home strip for four shillings and eleven.

You soon learned not to trust strangers.
Fair do's, Humpty Dumpty did look a bit of a barmpot,
but you didn't realise he had death wish.

So, next time you were sat on wall,
you kept your wits about you.

You learned that when shed began to creak
it were time to get out quick.

You learned not to kick football into old well shaft.

You learned when other kids began to run,
you should run too.

And you learned that meerkats don't have nine lives.
And that trams are very hard things.
Especially speeding ones.

Days Out And About

Don't get me wrong, we had our treats too. Me Uncle Ken and Auntie Norah would take us to Blackpool for day out.

Uncle Ken would cycle with us in back and Auntie Norah would take train.

Uncle Ken knew how much we enjoyed digging.
While we took it in turns to bury each other, Auntie Norah
would fetch a gallon pot of tea and a barrow of chips.

Sometimes we'd go off to zoo and tease komodo dragon.
He thought he were fast, but he were rubbish.

When it got windy we'd go up Bleak Hill and worry complete strangers by jumping onto their kites.

Mad Auntie Jess used to take me and me sister
up to municipal playground.

Slide were okay.

94

But I never got hang of them swings...

We Had Hobbies, Too

Music played a big part in our lives. Nobody in their right mind could resist the allure of the massed accordions of Saint Cuthbert's School Sinfonia.

And Cousin Stan could make old ladies weep with his rendition of 'Ilkley Moor Bah Tat'.

We enjoyed singing in the rain.
Which there was a lot of.

Reading the latest comics.

Or learning to swim. We didn't have swimming pools so they taught us in river. People will tell you 'meerkats don't like water'.

People are right.

Some Memorable Events From Childhood

There are moments that will always stick with you,
that you'll remember for rest of your life.

Like the day the king came to visit,
with man who played Dad in 'Mary Poppins'.

The first time you listened to a speech by
a member of the RMP, the Radical Meerkat Party,
and the great struggle for meerkat rights.

111

Or the day the town sewer flooded and
you found sixteen juicy slugs under half a barrel.

The day you got to play the cowboy instead of the Indian.

And the day you got to play real cowboys and Indians on a real horse, with a real dog...

...which if truth be known,
made you feel a little bit nervous.

Or the day a panda took your photo.
As they do...

Which was still a million times better than
the school photo you had done with clown.
They gave you option, you could have photo with
barn owl, clown or on your own.

Mum would have rung up school if we'd had a phone.

You remember the day that 'kissing machine' Doreen Braithwaite parked herself outside your front door and wouldn't go home till she snogged the living daylights out of you.

You remember your first real kiss that made your heart thump – when two tails became entwined.

And you remember that most special moment of all.
How could you ever forget it?

The day you sat in your first pedal car.
It didn't get much better than that...

Picture Credit Where
Picture Credit's Due

Other books in the series:

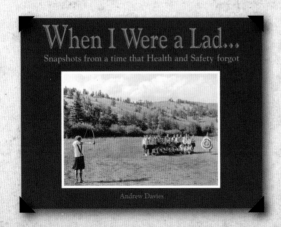

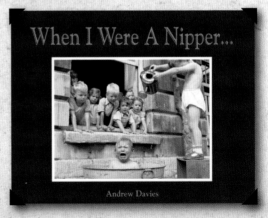